Dear Reader:

Windmill Hill quietly arrived in our offices from the author who was looking for a publisher. We read it, and we liked it so much that we decided we should publish it! We are proud of Windmill Hill, which is available only from the Weekly Reader Book Club.

Windmill Hill tells the story about two mice whose lives are touched by the humans who come to live at the old house on the hill. It is funny, touching, just a little scary, and happy. Write to us and tell us what you think of this book.

If you like animal stories, you might also like to read:

The Cricket In Times Square by George Selden
A Rat's Tale by Tor Seidler
The Wind In The Willows by Kenneth Grahame

Sincerely,

Stephen Fraser

Stephen Fraser
Senior Editor
Weekly Reader Books

Weekly Reader Book Club presents

WINDMILL HILL

by
Hope Slaughter Bryant
Illustrations by Pam Cote

NEWFIELD PUBLICATIONS

Middletown, Connecticut

This book is an original presentation of Newfield Publications, Inc.
Newfield Publications offers book clubs for children preschool through high school.
For further information write:
Newfield Publications, Inc. 4343 Equity Drive, Columbus, OH 43228.

Newfield Publications is a trademark of Newfield Publications, Inc.
Weekly Reader is a federally registered trademark of Weekly Reader Corporation.
Text copyright © 1992 Hope Slaughter.
Cover art and text illustrations © 1992 Newfield Publications, Inc.
Illustrations by Pam Cote.

Editor: Stephen Fraser
Designer: Vickie McTigue Kelly

ISBN #: 0-8374-9800-7
Printed in the United States of America.

For the Group
who loved Newly and Old Ragged
as much as I do.

1.

BACK TO THE HILL

Newly, a rather fat mouse, scurried along the edge of the broken stone wall. His heart was thumping. He felt all goose-bumpy. Back down the ditch at the side of the road, toward the gooseberry thicket, he dashed, and his mind raced as fast as his short legs ran. He had seen them and heard them. Old Ragged would be so surprised! His uncle had told him about the days, long ago, when there used to be humans living here on the hill.

He ducked into a small opening in the thorny bushes and plunged down the well-worn passageway to the nest. He burst in and nearly knocked Old Ragged over. "Uncle, Uncle! . . ." Newly stopped to puff. "Guess . . guess what!"

"My stars, Young One, what's gotten into you?" Old Ragged straightened his shoulders and brushed off his chest, though Newly hadn't actually bumped into him when he'd skidded to a stop.

Newly took a big gulp of air. "Humans, Uncle. I saw 'em." He had to stop for one more breath. "Humans up on the hill. I heard 'em talking, Uncle."

"Whoa, whoa, slow down. I can't understand a blasted thing if you keep gulping like that." Old Ragged shook his head. "Like I'm always telling you. Start at the beginning. And anyway," he added, "what's so exciting about humans? You've seen them before."

"Only once, Uncle, only once."

"Well, go on. Tell me about these." Old Ragged settled back into a comfortable position, which took a bit of doing with his old-age stiffness.

Newly was a little calmer by now. "Well," he began, "I was on my way home when I heard one of their machines humming. I watched, and it turned up the road toward the hill, so I followed along the ditch." A disapproving glance from his uncle made Newly add, "Of course, I was very careful."

"Humph," Old Ragged snorted.

"The machine was very loud," Newly continued, "and I think it was a dark sky color, though you could hardly tell because it was so splattered with mud. You know, the road up the hill is still very muddy from the spring thaw, and . . ."

Old Ragged tapped his paw on his knee. "Yes, yes, I know. You don't need to go back that far to begin your story."

"Well, when the machine got to the top of the hill, it stopped in front of the old farmhouse and a tall man jumped out, and he said things like, 'Smell that wonderful country air', and 'No people as far as you can see.' "

A spark of curiosity flared in Old Ragged's eyes. "Go on, go on."

"Then this woman got out, and she said, 'Oh, honey, isn't it a picture. So peaceful. And look at that quaint old windmill.' "

"And what's so quaint about that old windmill?" Ragged interrupted. "Hasn't pumped any water ever since the last human left. And that's been longer than I care to remember."

"But, Uncle," Newly went on, "I think they're coming to live here, then maybe it will."

"How's that?"

"Well, the lady got this sad look, and she said how she would miss Grandpa, but wasn't it just like him to leave this old house to them. Then the man put his arm around her and they went walking all around it."

"Humph," Ragged repeated.

"Uncle, maybe it will be like the old days—when there was a garden and the fields were planted. And if the windmill runs there'll be fresh water, and . . ."

"And," Old Ragged shook a stern finger, "there will be problems. Humans always mean problems. I haven't told you much about those."

"But Uncle . . ."

"They'll probably have a cat. And they'll set traps, and they'll have a way to . . ." Old Ragged wagged his head. "Never mind them. If people do come, just don't mind about them."

Newly understood the warning tone in Ragged's voice, and he dropped the subject of humans. Silently they took some pine nuts and gooseberries from their shrinking supply and had a bite of supper. When they had finished it was nearly dark, and Newly and Old Ragged curled up to sleep.

Still, it was difficult for Newly not to feel excited. He couldn't remember when there had been more than just the two of them on the hill. After the last humans left there were dry years, and most of the animals left too. Now the prospect of luscious, green vegetable gardens and whole fields of corn filled his head. Finally he fell asleep, but he dreamed and dreamed.

❦

Next morning, at the first streaks of light, Newly awoke with a start. Instead of the delicate whisper of wind rustling thick clumps of grass, he thought he heard creaking, then a faraway clanking. He got up quietly before Old Ragged stirred, and scurried down the passageway, out of the thicket. In the distance, up on the hill, he could see that the mud-splattered blue machine from the day before was still in front of the farmhouse.

He followed the ditch, as far as the stone wall, and scrambled up to have a better look. The same man was hammering on the rusty front doorknob. The lady was taking some boxes out of the car and stacking them on the porch.

Then, as Newly paused, watching and listening, he could hear water running! He scuttled across the wall and ran along its protecting edge as far as the yard.

He could see it now. Water was streaming

out of the pipe at the bottom of the windmill! The man called Honey must have taken the brake off, and the wind was gently turning the big weathered fan.

It was true! Newly was right! People were coming to live in the old farmhouse. He had to run and tell Old Ragged right away! As he raced along the edge of the road toward the stone wall, he heard the man call to the lady, "And let's call the place Windmill Hill, just like when Grandpa lived here."

II.
A Bit of Cheese

*T*he spring days grew warmer, and the afternoons lengthened. The gentle breeze on the hill was filled with the bustling sounds of things being done and tunes being whistled. Newly was drawn more and more to the hill, like metal to a magnet. He would sit for endless hours, concealed in a crack or crevice, taking in all the activities of these humans.

He watched the man called Honey brush a liquid on the old farmhouse. The front and half of one side now glowed with the creamy yellow color of dandelions. He watched the lady hang some filmy, white something in the front windows which she had scrubbed sparkling clean. There was a shiny new doorknob on the front door, and a new board over the hole in the front porch. But most exciting were all the wonderful new smells! Sweet, clean smells, fruity smells, smells that Newly couldn't imagine what or where they came from. He was entranced.

Of course, he didn't tell Old Ragged about the interesting things he saw and heard and smelled. On the day Newly came running in to announce that the humans were indeed here to stay, Old Ragged lectured again about the perils of people. "I can tell you stories, Young One," he said. "Stories that would curl your tail. You know, even your own mother was tempted by humans."

Newly's mother had died in some mysterious way. Old Ragged sometimes hinted at it but never fully explained. Newly sensed it must have been terrible. He didn't remember much about her, and he could never quite bring himself to ask.

When he did have to admit he'd been up on the hill, he was always quick to say how far away he stayed from the humans and how very carefully he concealed himself. Old

Ragged "Humphed" a lot and said very little.

Newly's favorite place to sit was under the big pipe at the bottom of the windmill. He loved the rushing sound, and it was fascinating to watch the clear water steadily pour out into the big trough. He'd never seen so much water!

On one particular day, when Newly was taking a drink from the fresh puddle under the pipe, the most heavenly smell reached out and tickled his nose! It was almost as if this wonderful odor was a part of his memory, but the memory wouldn't come back to him.

Newly scooted across the yard to get closer to the house, which he was sure had to be the source of that smell. He spotted the man in the side yard, moving dirt around, lifting it with a long stick that had a metal piece on the end. Newly darted under the hedge that ran along the back of the house and listened to the man hum as he scraped and dug. He had to find out what that smell was!

It was strong on this side of the house.

From his hiding place under the hedge, he could see the back porch. Next to the back door was an open window. One of the filmy white things hanging there fluttered in the breeze, a perfect cover for the momentary shadow of a passing mouse. Ever so softly but ever so quickly, Newly was up on the windowsill and down the other side into the house. A giant, black iron hulk squatted in one corner, and Newly whisked behind one of its bulgy legs. A sizzling noise came from its top. It was the very place the smell was coming from!

Newly's heart pounded hard in his crouching body. He heard a padding noise, then saw feet walking toward him. Panic was about to overcome him when the feet turned and walked to some spindly-looking wooden objects in the middle of the room.

Newly let out a tiny bit of breath. He heard metal tinkling, then water splashing. More padding, then the screen door slammed. "Honey," the lady's voice called, "Can you stop for lunch now? I made some grilled cheese sandwiches."

Cheese. Why did that sound so strangely familiar? He had to taste cheese. He had to!

Feet walked in again, four this time. Water splashed again. Legs appeared, as the man and lady pulled out the wooden things and sat down on them. "How's the garden coming?" the lady asked.

"Pretty good," said the man called Honey. "Should be in by now, though. Hope I can finish turning today."

Newly listened to them talk about things called curtains and canning, then he lost his concentration. He strained his ears to hear what was moving outside the window. A mockingbird called, and a fly buzzed against the glass. He was growing very tired of waiting motionless.

Then, *scrape, scrape,* the man stood up. "Good lunch, Sweetheart," he said. "I'd better get back to work."

"Let me see what you've already done,"

Sweetheart said, as her feet followed the man's across the room and out the door.

Now. Newly quickly stretched to uncramp his legs, darted over to the middle of the room, hurdled himself up on one of the wooden things, then leaped up onto the cloth above. There were the remains of what Honey had called lunch. Crusty, wheat-tasting bits and the source of that smell—cheese.

Newly had never nibbled so fast! He only dared a few seconds. He crammed all he could into his fat cheek pouches, leaped down, crossed the floor like a streak, scrambled up and out the window, then plunged down into the hedge.

He waited until his sides had stopped heaving, then hurried along under the hedge to the end of the house and made a dash across the yard to the old stone wall. Once safely in its shadow, he began to really taste the stolen goods.

The cheese was more wonderful than he could have even imagined! Smooth and

buttery and indescribable. He savored every morsel, then squealed with delight! Very satisfied with his own cleverness, he ambled toward home, swaggering with the heady discovery of the humans' lunch of cheese.

Old Ragged was resting at the entrance to the passageway, soaking up some sun. Newly tried to hide his smile, but that wasn't what gave him away.

"Cheese. Your whiskers smell like cheese," Old Ragged exclaimed with disgust.

Newly was speechless.

"And in broad daylight. You got some of the humans' cheese in the daytime!" Ragged's voice grew louder and harsher as he wagged his paw in Newly's face. "And now that you've tasted it, you'll never be satisfied without it again. Never!"

Newly hung his head.

Old Ragged turned his back on Newly and started down the path, grumbling. "Your mother was foolish, too. Used to sing that meaningless rhyme to you about your name and cheese."

Newly's mind clicked. That's what was buried deep in his memory—the song his mother used to sing to him before she died.

"Newly Born, oh, Newly Born,
Little baby mine,
If you please, a bit more cheese,
Oh, little baby mine."

Newly guessed it was a meaningless rhyme, but at least now he knew the meaning of cheese!

III.
THE INCINERATOR

No matter how Old Ragged had scolded, Newly just couldn't help himself. He couldn't stay away from the hill. He couldn't wait to see what new developments each day would bring. The whole house was a soft yellow color now, and the new garden in the side yard was beginning to sprout. He had learned many things about the humans from overhearing their conversations.

One morning, when Newly was listening from his favorite spot on a small ledge that ran along the foundation under the window, he heard the lady called Sweetheart complain, "But, Honey, I know I left it right here on the kitchen sink, and I can't find it anywhere!"

"Now, Sweetheart," Honey answered, "it must be here somewhere. Let's look again. Are you sure this is where you left it?"

Sweetheart's voice trembled. "Well, I think so. I took it off and put it here when I did the dishes. Oh, I just can't have lost it."

There were no wonderful smells floating out the kitchen window, and Newly sensed the conversation was somehow unhappy, so he left his post and slipped through the morning shadows to the backyard. He had planned to check the trash in the incinerator first thing.

Newly had watched Honey replace some of the broken stones in the big square burner, then oil and repair the sagging door on the front. He would let trash accumulate inside for a few days before setting it on fire. The door was usually ajar, unless of course, the trash was being burned.

Sorting through these human scraps was a source of great pleasure to Newly. He had found a variety of edibles, mostly good tasting, and a number of other interesting things—shiny round tin things, empty paper boxes, and pieces of cloth. He'd even saved a small scrap of blue flannel, just right for curling up on. He'd hidden it under the hedge, though. No telling how angry Old Ragged would get if he discovered it in the nest.

Today Newly was pleased to see the incinerator door entirely open, and soon he was sorting through the big sack of trash stuffed in the front. He had a few licks of butter from a wrapper, found a bit of cracker, and was about to pull on a banana peel, when a shiny round object caught his eye. He pawed it out of some papers to have a better look. Its soft golden luster glowed as it caught the sunlight. Suddenly, Sweetheart's words from a few minutes earlier came back to him: *"Oh, I just can't have lost it!"*

This beautiful gold circle could be what she had lost, could be what was upsetting her so. The more he thought about it, the more Newly was sure it must be. He pulled it free of the trash and dragged it along the stones of the incinerator. It wasn't that large, but it was heavy.

At the edge, he gave it a push and it dropped to the ground. He scooted down after it, then began first to pull, then to push it across the yard. It was more than he had bargained for, and he was soon panting and had to stop and rest.

After a short while, he heaved and tugged some more and finally shoved it under the hedge. He had to rest again. He could barely lift this heavy gold circle. He could never carry it in his teeth long enough to go up over the windowsill and into the house. And he certainly could never return it to what Sweetheart had called the kitchen sink.

Newly squatted gloomily under the hedge. Too bad he couldn't ask Old Ragged for some help. He would know what to do. Or maybe he wouldn't, since he refused to have anything to do with humans and their problems.

Newly stared at the rich hue of the golden circle. Maybe it would fit around his neck. With no more thought to the matter, he hoisted it with both paws and poked his head through its shininess. It worked! Like a heavy yoke, the ring rested on his plump shoulders. He staggered a bit under its sudden weight, then righted himself, pleased with his inspiration.

Newly made his way slowly along the edge of the back porch to the window, which was open, as usual. It had been difficult enough to run up the side of the house before. Could he do it with his burden? He hesitated briefly, then scrambled up as best he could, straining to grab a foothold on each board, slipping back, pulling up again. Finally, he reached the sill. He huddled in the corner of the window behind the folds of filmy white cloth.

Now, where to put it, he wondered. He remembered Sweetheart had said she left it on the kitchen sink, and he thought that was what they ran the water in, but the shiny surface looked very slippery. Maybe just put it on the cupboard top here below the window, he thought.

The sound of a whirring machine starting up somewhere in the back of the house made up his mind quickly for him. He put both paws up to his shoulders and tugged hard at the gold ring. It popped off his head like a cork out of a bottle and went sailing through the air, then bounced and clinked as it rolled across the floor. Newly didn't wait to see where it came to rest. He was out the window, down the side of the house, across the porch, and safely under the hedge before he even took a breath.

And with no time to spare. Honey's big shoes went by the hedge just moments after Newly had ducked in. Newly scrootched up tiny and waited, getting his breath back and thinking how close he had probably come to disaster.

He heard the screen door slam, then water running and Honey humming. Then Honey called, "Sweetheart, Sweetheart, come here."

After a moment, he heard Sweetheart exclaim, "Oh, Honey! Where'd you find it?

Oh, I'm so glad!"

Newly supposed they were holding on to each other. He had seen them do this often. Honey said, "It must have fallen on the floor. I found it right here by the table leg."

"Oh, thank goodness," said Sweetheart. She sounded much happier.

And for some reason, Newly had a warm, happy feeling, too.

IV.
CATS AND KIDS

"And do be careful. I just don't trust that old car anymore," Sweetheart said. She stood on the porch watching Honey get into the old blue car. "If I know Matilda, there will be quite a few to choose from."

It was sunrise, and Newly listened from the shadow of the water trough. He had crept out of the nest very early so he wouldn't have to face Old Ragged's hard looks.

"Matilda always has healthy litters. They're probably running around everywhere by now," Honey said. He closed the door and rolled down the window. "I'll be back before dark. Don't worry."

The car clunked away down the hill. Sweetheart went into the house. Newly took a long drink from the puddle by the trough. He wished, as he often did, that he understood more of the human's words. Why was the man going away, and what was a matilda? Well, the man wouldn't be working in the garden today, so Newly could sample all of the young budding plants with no worry.

He whisked around to the garden and proceeded to get very full. Then he felt very guilty. He kept thinking of Old Ragged, who ate only from their meager store of berries and seeds, and would have nothing to do with the humans on the hill.

The summer mornings got hotter earlier now, and Newly felt uncomfortably stuffed and warm. He crossed the yard to the shade under the hedge and curled up on his piece of blue flannel.

It was late afternoon when he was awakened by the chugging sound of the human's machine pulling up the hill. He scurried around the edge of the house to the front just in time to see it stop in a swirl of dust. Honey jumped out, then lifted out a large wicker basket.

Sweetheart had heard it too, and she hurried down the porch steps to peer into the basket. "Oh, let me see! Oh, look . . . Ohhhhhh . . . isn't it precious?"

Newly was overcome with curiosity. What on earth was it? He darted into the shadow at the edge of the porch and watched Sweetheart reach down into the basket. She lifted out a tiny, fuzzy gray thing and set it on the ground. It wobbled over to sniff at the tip of Sweetheart's shoe. Newly's heart thumped against his chest when he heard its soft mewings in between Sweetheart's oooooooos and ohhhhhhhhs. A baby cat. Which would obviously grow, every day, into a big cat. Newly's stomach felt upside down. He had heard Old Ragged's many stories about the old tom cat that used to come around the hill hunting, and they weren't pleasant ones.

He sat tentatively for a while in the twilight shadows, too curious to leave but knowing he should. Just when he had convinced himself to start for home, he heard the unfamiliar drone of a machine. It didn't chug or sputter, but hummed evenly. He waited to see what it would be.

A different-looking machine, shiny and long, pulled up in front of the house and stopped. Unconsciously, Newly scrunched up small; he watched two humans get out—a man and a woman— then a little human. The small one tugged at a large brightly-colored bag that was in the backseat, until the bag landed with a thud at her feet. Sweetheart waved and called, "Hi! You made it! Did you have any trouble finding us?"

The woman held onto Sweetheart a moment, then said, "No, not at all. And isn't this wonderful—way out in the country and everything!" She turned to the small human and nudged her forward. "Alexandra, say hello to your aunt and uncle."

The little one muttered something Newly couldn't hear and hovered close to the woman's legs.

"Alexandra," Sweetheart said, bending

down and giving her a pat, "see what we got just this afternoon." She lifted the wiggly gray ball of fur into the small human's arms. "Isn't it adorable?"

Newly watched intently. The little human must be an Alexandra. Her eyes grew wide and she smiled as she clutched the little cat to her chest. "It really is," she said shyly. "Ohhhh, it's so tiny— and so soft."

Newly's heart was thumping hard again. Baby cats, small humans—what next?

V.
A HOUSE FOR A MOUSE

Newly avoided the farmhouse for a while, especially the front porch with the big wicker basket in one corner. He passed by carefully only on visits to the incinerator or the water trough. But, as the days passed, it was harder and harder to ignore his interest in the small human he'd heard them call Alexandra. The sleek, shiny machine had been on the hill only one day, and when it left, the small human had stayed behind with Sweetheart and Honey.

His curiosity finally won out, and Newly began watching Alexandra whenever he could. She spent a lot of time outdoors with the baby cat. She stroked it, pulled a string through the grass for it to chase, and even dressed it up in little clothes. When she wasn't doing something to the cat, she was cradling and humming to things that looked like baby humans wrapped up in cloth.

Soon Newly had scratched out a comfortable place under the woodpile so he could watch the side yard better. Every day, Alexandra did something that intrigued him. She spread colored water on big sheets of paper. She made bright colors on paper with waxy sticks. She brought out a furry thing Newly thought was the shape of a bear, and she put clothes on that too.

But what he loved watching her do the most was fuss around with a little house—a perfectly wonderful little house. She would carry it out to the yard and set it under the willow tree. It was the color of summer blue sky, with little pieces of cloth at the windows, just like in the big house. It had a door, even a front step. She had miniature humans that seemed to be stiff, like they were made of wood, and she would put them in and take them out of the house and talk to them all afternoon. Newly had never imagined there could be such a beautiful house, just the size for a mouse. He wanted to go inside so badly he could hardly stand it.

As Newly watched one day, Alexandra brought the house outside and set it under the tree as usual. In a short while, Honey appeared with two long poles and a metal box. "Okay, Alexandra," he said. "I'm finished in the garden. We can go now. We'll drive over to Peavine Bridge and see if they're biting there today."

"All right," Alexandra exclaimed, jumping up. They went around to the front of the house together, got in the old blue car, and drove away down the hill.

There was that lovely little house, and no one around at all. Trembling with antici-pation, Newly scampered across the yard and cautiously pushed on the front door. It opened smoothly, and he peeked in. His heart thumped. He was face-to-face with two tiny humans that stared blankly at him. He stood frozen to the spot, staring back. Then, just before he turned to run, he remembered. These were only the wooden things Alexandra put in and took out of the house all the time. Relief washed over him, and he scooted inside and looked around.

The house was divided up into boxes like the big house was, and there were many objects like there were in Sweetheart's house—things to sit on, eat on, and sleep on, just like he'd seen the humans do. Although some of the things were a bit small for him, he tried them all. He propped himself up in a chair. He lay down for a moment on the bed. Newly had never been so thrilled with anything before! He scurried excitedly around and around, exploring every nook and corner.

When Newly in his delight whisked by the front door for the tenth time, he happened to glance up for just an instant. Two intense yellow eyes watched his every move from the doorway. He suddenly went limp all over. He had totally forgotten about the cat!

It was a few long moments before he could convince his legs to move again. He kicked the little door closed and scooted into a corner at the back of the house. In a moment, there was a loud *kalump* on the roof that shook everything. Then a furry gray tail appeared, hanging down over the nearest window. It began to switch rhythmically back and forth. Newly huddled in his corner, still breathless. The cat was on the roof.

Minutes seemed like hours. Newly concentrated hard on not panicking. He could outlast the cat's patience if the cat couldn't get any closer to him than this. And that didn't seem likely. All the openings were too small for a cat. He thought of Old Ragged, wisely refusing to go close to humans and their things. And he was right, of course. What a mess Newly had gotten himself into this time. He felt forlorn and utterly stupid, and his legs already had cramps in them.

After what seemed like a very long time,

Newly was jarred out of his numb, waiting state by Alexandra's voice, calling across the yard. "Kitty, kitty, kitty." Newly came to full attention. "Kitty, kitty, here kitty. Oh, there you are."

Alexandra was very close now. Newly heard a scraping sound on the roof. "Silly kitty. Trying to play with my doll house. You won't fit, you know." Her voice began to move away in the direction of the big house. "Come on, I'll feed you, silly thing."

Newly edged out of his corner to stretch. What a glorious feeling—to be able to move again. His aching legs wobbled under him as he went to the front door. It was closed, tight. He pushed it with his nose, then with his two front paws, then with his whole weight behind his shoulder. It wouldn't budge. He was still trapped.

The only way out was through one of the little windows on the side. He pulled himself up to the nearest one and poked his head out. Then he pawed with his hind legs to push himself through. Halfway out, the bulge of his stomach stuck. He had been eating too well lately.

He pushed and pushed with his hind legs. He could feel himself moving a bit, but the sides of the window were scraping and tearing at his fur. With another very hard push, Newly fell to the ground outside with a plop.

His sides and his stomach stung, and his legs still ached. He half-hobbled, half-ran to the hedge. As soon as he had rested a minute he would go directly to the comfort of his nest and never, never come up to the hill again.

VI.
A SURPRISE VISIT

"What in heaven's name happened to the fur around your middle, Young One?" Old Ragged asked that evening. "Something to do with those humans up on the hill no doubt." His voice was gruff, but there was a hint of sympathy in his eyes.

Newly didn't answer directly. "It's nothing, really," he said. "Just a few scratches."

"Humph," his uncle said. "Someday you'll learn."

I have, I have, Newly thought to himself.

And he had, for now. He was determined not have any more close calls. He took long naps, tidied up around the nest more often, and spent more time collecting food. He could tell Old Ragged was pleased with the increase in their larder, even though he didn't say so.

One morning, as he stepped out of the passageway into the sunlight, Newly thought he heard talking. He looked up the road, and there was Alexandra, with the baby cat trailing behind her, coming down the hill toward the gooseberry thicket. She was chattering away to the cat, as usual, which always seemed odd to Newly, because the cat couldn't answer back.

As they came closer, Newly could just catch some of what she was saying: ". . . don't you think that's a good idea? And we'll catch them in this big jar."

Catch them? In a big jar? Panic seized him. Catch them in a big jar! How did she know where he was? How could she know? And Ragged. They must be after Old Ragged too.

They were approaching the thicket now, and Newly could hear every word. "And I punched little holes in the lid so they can breathe until we're ready to use them. Won't it be a good surprise?"

Newly shuttered. Use them? For what? She must have seen him the day he had been in her little house. Now his foolishness had endangered Old Ragged, too.

Newly drew back into the passageway just as Alexandra's shadow passed over the bushes near the entrance. He flattened himself on the smooth dirt floor, and the thumping of his heart echoed in his ears.

He heard feet crackling in the dry weeds just outside, then rustling in the bushes. "I'll bet there's millions of them in these bushes," he heard Alexandra say.

Newly scooted farther back in the tunnel. Old Ragged was asleep. He had to protect him from the terrible fate of being trapped in a jar. His frantic mind seized on the first plan that came to him. He would lead them away from the nest. He'd get the cat to chase him; Alexandra would chase the cat; and Ragged would be safe.

It took several seconds to gather all his courage. Then he ran down the passage to the outside. He popped out from under the thick bushes just a few mouse steps from the toe of a shoe! He dodged it in the nick of time, then plunged into some tall weeds beyond.

He saw Alexandra standing only a few yards away, holding up the big jar and searching around in the bushes. He spotted the baby cat across the road, crouched on its haunches, watching a butterfly hover near some sunflowers.

"Ouch! These bushes are prickly!" Alexandra complained. *Hah,* he said quietly to himself. *Serves you right.*

Now for his plan. His breathing was almost back to normal. If he could just quiet his pounding heart, he would run up the road, right in front of the cat.

He heard a clink. "Got another one. That makes eight." Alexandra was putting something into that big jar and slamming the top on.

Eight? Eight what? If she had already caught eight somethings, maybe she wasn't here to catch him after all. He held himself very still in the weeds.

He watched as Alexandra stepped out of the bushes. "There," she said, "That's enough. Now we're all ready to go fishing this afternoon." She started walking back up the road, calling, "Kitty, kitty, here kitty. Come on, kitty." The baby cat finished batting at the sunflowers and ambled over to her.

Newly held his breath as they passed by him. Just as he was silently letting his breath go, Alexandra stopped. She set the shiny glass jar on the ground, then stooped over and did something with strings on the top of her shoe.

Newly was eyeball-to-eyeball with lots of hopping, crawling grasshoppers trapped in the shiny jar. She had been catching grasshoppers!

Newly watched as she picked up the jar, stood up, and skipped off up the road. He relaxed his position and shook his head in disbelief. There was no predicting what humans might do next.

VII.

GOOD FORTUNE OR NOT?

*A*s the days went by, Newly thought more and more about the garden and about those long cool drinks from the puddle by the trough. Finally, he decided to make a trip over to Rapid Creek. He arrived at its bank after a long hike, only to discover that barely a trickle of water was running over its stony bottom. On his way home, gloom set in. Life had certainly become dull and unexciting— actually boring.

Later, when he heard a smoothly humming human machine in the distance, he couldn't hold off his old curiosity any longer. And he was running along in the ditch at the side of the road anyway, so he stopped and waited to have a look.

The long, shiny car that had come before purred up to the house, and the same man and woman got out. Newly darted up the ditch in time to see Alexandra come bursting out of the screen door. "Mommy, Daddy! Did you bring me a surprise?" She ran to the man and woman. They held her and patted her and fussed over her.

"Alexandra, you've grown two inches!" the lady exclaimed. "And look how tan you are. You look wonderful!"

They went into the house, all talking at once. Newly stayed safely under the far end of the hedge, but he could hear their excited talk and laughter floating out the farmhouse window.

Well, he wouldn't go close enough to hear what they were saying inside, but while he was here and they were all inside, he'd stop by the garden just long enough for a little something.

Some of the corn and tomatoes had been picked. The cucumber and bean vines were still quite full, though, and there were lettuces, cabbages, radishes, and onions. After a satisfying snack and a cool drink from the puddle under the windmill trough, Newly made his way back along the hedge, then skittered into the shadow of the old stone wall. He heard voices again, and the car door slamming. He scrambled up on the wall for a look.

The man was talking to Honey as they loaded some bundles and bags into the long, shiny car. "Thanks again," he said. "It's been such a great vacation for Alexandra."

The lady came out of the house, followed by Alexandra and Sweetheart. "Yes, Alexandra had the best time—such a good experience for her," the lady said.

"And thanks a lot for Fluffy," Alexandra piped up. She was carrying the large wicker basket to the car. Newly perked up his ears.

"Yes," said the lady, "are you sure now? You really want to give up your new kitten?"

Sweetheart patted Alexandra's head. "She's become so attached to it, I'd hate to separate them. We can get another one."

"Well, she's sure thrilled with that kitty," the man said, holding on to Sweetheart for a moment. Then everyone took turns holding on to everyone.

"Oh, wait a minute," said Honey, and he ran into the house. He came back quickly, carrying a bag. "Some fresh vegetables from the garden. A little bit of the country to take home with you."

The man took the bag and held out his hand. Honey shook it up and down. "We can't wait to come back. It's a wonderful spot."

"Anytime," Sweetheart said. "Anytime. We'd love to have you."

By now the man, lady, Alexandra, and the basket were all in the car. After door slamming and many shouted good-byes, the long, shiny car wound its way down the hill. Newly watched until all he could see was a tiny trailing cloud of dust. Honey and Sweetheart watched, too. Then they put their arms around each other and walked back into the house.

Life had certainly taken a turn for the better. No girl, no cat, no tempting little house. Things would be as they were when he started to watch the humans. Now there was really no reason to stay away from the hill. Newly felt an overwhelming sense of happiness as he ambled back down the ditch to the gooseberry thicket at the bottom of the hill.

If only Old Ragged could share some of this good feeling, he thought, as he scooted through the small opening in the bushes. Maybe if he could somehow convince Old Ragged to venture out more, he might eventually even get him to go up to the garden.

Newly was almost to the end of the passageway. It seemed very quiet and vacant. "Ragged," he called, as he came into the nest. "Ragged, Old Ragged." No *humph* answered. No cough. No clearing of a raspy throat.

Newly looked everywhere, even to the end of the escape passageway. No Ragged, anywhere.

His heart gave a quick beat. Old Ragged hardly ever left the gooseberry bushes. Where could he be?

VIII.
THAT OLD CURIOSITY

*T*heir comfortable nest under the tangle of gooseberry bushes had always seemed so cozy and safe to Newly. Now as he sat awake in the dark, worrying about Old Ragged, it wasn't the same at all. Where could he be? What had happened to him? Newly couldn't stop thinking about all the things that might have happened.

The muffled hoot of an owl, no doubt on his way home after a night of hunting, made Newly shiver. He stretched his tired, stiff body. Better go out and look some more before daylight.

He scooted down the passageway and out into the fading moonlight. Going in ever larger circles, he searched farther and farther away from the thicket. He sniffed until his nose hurt. He listened for the faintest noises. He studied every shadow carefully. But there was no clue as to Old Ragged's whereabouts.

Discouraged and heavy hearted, he watched the sky streak with the rosy glow of dawn. Mist was slowly rising off the meadow. Maybe a drink of water or something to eat would make him feel better. He headed up the ditch toward the hill. Arriving at the hedge, he stopped and listened for any familiar sound. His forlorn, all-alone feeling made him want to hear some sign of life, even the humans' voices. But everything was gray stillness.

Suddenly, Newly thought he heard a low moaning sound coming from somewhere in the side yard. He concentrated with all his senses to pinpoint the place the murmuring voice was coming from. It sounded like somewhere under the willow tree.

Newly cautiously made his way around the side of the house until he could see the huge tree. For one moment he thought something very small moved on the ground in the ghostly shadows of its overhanging branches, but he couldn't be sure. He crouched, waiting and listening, his heart beating fast. There it was again. He would have to go closer to see what it was. Or maybe if he waited . . . But it was growing lighter every minute, and soon whatever it was would be able to see him too.

As he hesitated, trying to decide, Newly heard a weak but very familiar cough. It was Old Ragged's, without a doubt!

Newly whisked across the lawn, plunged into the shadows of the willow tree, and almost stumbled over the form of his uncle, huddled in the grass. "Old Ragged, is that you?"

"What an idiotic question. Of course it's me," came the husky reply.

"But, what are you doing here?"

"I can tell you all that later. The important thing now is to get out of here."

"Yes, right," nodded Newly, still staring in amazement at his uncle.

"The problem is my front leg. Caught it in a vine or in something. Anyway, I tripped. Must have twisted it. When I got up, I couldn't stand on the confounded thing."

Newly leaned down to have a look. "Here.

Put your good leg around my shoulders." He helped Old Ragged straighten up. "Now, hold on to me and try to hop."

Old Ragged hoisted himself to his hind feet and leaned heavily on Newly. Slowly they began to walk-hop back across the lawn. Old Ragged breathed hard, and they stopped often to rest. Daylight was coming fast now, and Newly was nervous. His mind was spinning with questions, but they would have to wait.

By the time they stopped under the hedge, Old Ragged was panting and wheezing. Newly released Old Ragged's arm gently, then ran off for a moment, returning with the piece of blue flannel. He spread it out. Without a word, Old Ragged settled down into its comforting softness.

They huddled in silence for some time. Newly tried hard not to push for explanations until Old Ragged was ready. Finally he asked, "Uncle, does your leg hurt a lot?"

"Throbs. Aches. But could be worse."

There was another long silence. Then Old

Ragged cleared his throat. "Just had to see for myself. Tried and tried to pay no attention to all the comin' and goin' and commotion. Did, too, for a long time."

Newly said nothing. He didn't want to interrupt Old Ragged's story.

"Then one day I was following the road, minding my own business," Ragged went on, seeming more willing to talk now. "I didn't intend to go up the hill, but then this feelin' came so strong. Something made me want to see for myself, just once."

Newly nodded. "I know, Uncle. I know."

"Well, I saw all right. Amazing things. And once wasn't enough. Then I had to come up every day."

Newly nodded some more. "That's the way it was with me, too, Uncle."

There was another silence, then Newly asked, "Did you see the little house, Uncle?"

"Yup. Never did get a chance to go in. The day I saw it under that old willow tree the human child was fiddling with it, then she took it away." Old Ragged shifted his

position and gave a little moan.

"You all right, Uncle?" asked Newly anxiously.

"Suppose I will be."

"I went into that house," Newly said. "That's how I tore my fur and scraped up my middle. The door stuck, and I had to climb out the window."

"Figured it was something like that." Ragged shook his head. "Well, I can see how you'd want to."

After a moment Newly asked, "Were you coming up to the hill again when you tripped and fell?"

"Yes, and now look at me." Ragged's slumped shoulders and bent head made Newly feel sorry he had asked.

"Well, you'll be safe here, Uncle. I can bring you food. I can even make a nest. Then when your leg is better we can go home."

Old Ragged coughed, then cleared his throat. "Can't think of any better plan for now, Young One."

IX.
THE DECISION

*I*t wasn't difficult for Newly to get a supply of food to Old Ragged in his spot under the hedge. Newly made many trips to the garden and loaded his cheek pouches with corn kernels, seeds, and bits of sweet roots. Water was a different matter. He had to place leaves near Old Ragged's bed on the flannel, cup them up, and hope for heavy dew.

It was actually a comfortable spot, though—a good vantage point from which to observe the house. Now that Newly had reason to suspect Old Ragged was as interested in the humans as he was.

There was a lot of activity to watch. Honey often took the old car and returned with the back loaded down with wood. He sawed the wood into pieces and stacked it on the wood-pile until it nearly covered the south side of the house. Sweetheart stayed in the house most of the time, but they could sometimes hear her humming, even singing. Some days, rows of glass jars lined the windowsills or the back porch, sparkling in the sun. They were filled with tomatoes, beans, cucumbers, and other things Newly didn't know.

The second day under the hedge, while they were having some fresh corn kernels and a bit of cabbage, Old Ragged had said, almost casually, " That other human wasn't like these two."

"What was he like, Uncle?" Newly prodded. He had a very sketchy picture of those long-ago times.

"Actually, I saw very little of him. He didn't work outside much. But he had a foolish dog that barked all the time."

"Did the dog chase you?"

"He chased everything that moved, but he yipped all the while, so hc never caught anything."

"But you told me there was a garden then,

and water."

"True, there was, but small. Not like this one. And cats. There were cats. I don't know how many. Always prowling around. I didn't even try coming up here."

His uncle knew more about humans than Newly had realized, and he was about to ask more questions, but Old Ragged had put on his "I'm through talking about it" expression, so he didn't bother.

Still, the next day, after Old Ragged had hobbled around some by himself and he was resting, he brought it up again. "He looked different from these humans, too. He had white hair on his face, and he leaned on a stick when he walked."

"He must have looked very odd," Newly encouraged.

"No, not really odd, but rather sad."

"What ever happened to him, Uncle?"

"I don't know. One day he just wasn't there anymore, or the dog and cats either. The windmill stopped pumping. What was left of the garden dried up. Pretty soon all the other animals left, too."

Thinking about all of this made Newly feel somehow sad, too, but he didn't say anything.

In a few more days, Old Ragged could walk slowly up and down under the hedge several times a day. The crisp autumn air made Newly scurry even faster than usual to gather food for them. The days were growing shorter, and some mornings there was a dusting of frost on the grass, but neither of them talked about returning to their nest in the gooseberry thicket yet.

"Uncle," Newly said one day, as he darted under the hedge, trying to keep the excitement out of his voice, "I've found the best place for us to spend the winter. It will be dry and warm, and we won't have to worry about snow or ice."

"Where have you been exploring now, Young One?" There was a hint of affection in Old Ragged's voice. He rarely disapproved of Newly's discoveries anymore.

"It's under the back porch. Do you think you can walk that far, Uncle?"

"Suppose I could give it a try—around twilight. To the back of the house here?"

"Yes, not very far at all. There's a hole. I'll show you."

Later, as they hurried across the small stretch of grass that separated the end of the hedge from the back porch, Newly discovered that Old Ragged could really move quite well by now. He led the way along the base of the porch to the side and disappeared into a small hole near the ground. Old Ragged followed without objection.

There was a bit of daylight still coming in through two small screened openings on this side of the foundation, but they didn't need much light. Their senses told them all they needed to know. The damp, earthy smell was a familiar one. The beams and boards of the porch were about a foot above the hard-packed dirt.

"This is a snug, warm spot, all right,"

Old Ragged agreed, "but maybe a bit too near them."

"But we can get outside in a second if we need to, and look at all the room to store things!" Newly could hardly talk fast enough. "We'll bring the nest from under the hedge— even the flannel, then we can start bringing food from the garden before it's all gone. We can . . ."

"I don't know," Old Ragged interrupted. "We'd have to move fast. I'm not much good at running yet."

But Newly chattered on. "Of course, we'll have to be quiet, but that won't bother us any, and we can hear when they're around. There'll be . . ."

"Wait, Young One," Old Ragged interrupted again, "it sounds very fine, but living this close all the time is just bound to cause problems."

"But Uncle," Newly stopped, and his whiskers twitched as he sniffed the air.

"I understand how you like to watch them.

But moving underneath them?" Old Ragged began to sniff, too.

"Uncle, just smell that!" Newly exclaimed. Lovely browning, cooking smells filled the air.

"Hmmmm, well, we could try it for a while. See if it's as good as we think." Old Ragged scratched his chin and took another long breath of the wonderful new smell. "It might be good—just might be good."

X.

A MIRACLE

*O*ne frosty morning when Newly woke up he had a feeling something had changed in the night. He darted over to the small hole at the base of the porch and poked his head out. The quiet, white world outside took his breath away. Large, soft flakes were still falling lazily. First snowfalls always seemed so wondrous to him. And this time he and his uncle had been so cozy they hadn't even known it was snowing!

Old Ragged stirred and was soon stretching. His injured front leg had healed nicely, and his mood seemed to improve with each day. Sometimes Newly got the urge to pat him and tell him how glad he was to have him for an uncle. But, he never did.

This day they would spend inside and avoid any tell tale tracks in the fresh snow.

There was plenty to keep them busy. Hastily gathered food had to be sorted and stacked, bits of this and that had to be shredded and added to the nest. Newly could not remember ever feeling so contented.

Both of them had grown accustomed to the sounds and smells of the humans just above them. They could tell Sweetheart's soft footsteps from Honey's heavier ones, and the muted murmur of voices had become the normal background of each day. They also had many favorite smells, though they didn't have the slightest idea what most of them were.

So winter went pleasantly. Newly listened patiently to Old Ragged's stories and actually enjoyed most of them. And in a somehow more accepting way, Old Ragged sometimes even asked Newly for his opinion. They talked and talked about many things.

Several times it was on the tip of Newly's tongue to ask more about his mother, but something still made him hesitate. He guessed Old Ragged was all the family he had ever really needed anyway.

The network of tunnels they dug in the now deep snow gave them exercise and somewhat fresher air. Other than these, they had not tried, or even talked about trying, to go beyond the comfort of their spot under the porch. Newly had noticed tiny cracks and spaces here and there from time to time, but, being so satisfied, hadn't had the urge to explore any of them.

For some reason, lately, there seemed to be a growing air of hustle and bustle above them. There were more voices, more music, more stomping out into the snow, and more especially delicious smells—sweet smells. All this activity made Newly and Old Ragged sense excitement and anticipation, though they didn't know for what. And then, of course, it roused the old curiosities.

"We just need to take one little look at what's going on up there these days, Uncle," Newly remarked one morning.

"Don't know about that," replied his uncle.

"From the sounds of it, they're always around up there."

"Not at night," persisted Newly. "The moon is nearly full, so there's bound to be moonlight in the house."

"Hmmmmmm," Ragged mused. "Suppose it would be safe?"

"In the middle of the night? Why not?" Newly felt a new confidence now that his uncle considered his opinion worthwhile. "Let's go up tonight. I'll see if I can find a crack big enough."

"Hmmmmmm," Ragged repeated. But he didn't disagree.

Newly set to work carefully exploring the floor above them where it joined the house. With a chew here and there he knew he could find a way.

Later, when all was quiet, and the hour was well into the night, Newly showed Old Ragged the opening he had found, and enlarged a bit. It was tight, but they used mouse techniques of making themselves thin and tiny. They came up into the room Newly had visited the day he discovered cheese, and ever so silently and slowly made their way along the wall. There seemed to be a glow coming from the next room and they crept cautiously in its direction.

Neither of them was prepared for what they saw when they came to the doorway. Both stopped, unable to move, and stared.

Newly was the first to recover his voice. "Uncle," he said weakly, "look what they've done to that tree. Isn't it wonderful?"

"It's the most beautiful thing I've ever seen in all my years," Old Ragged answered with reverence in his crackly voice. "In all my years . . ." he repeated quietly.

A tall, straight fir tree towered above them, glowing with tiny white lights that reflected in glittering silver ropes and long streaming silver icicles. Silver balls hung from some of the fullest branches, twinkling back at them. Bright colored boxes with silver and gold ribbons tied around them were tucked under the lowest branches.

"And underneath—look under the tree," Newly said, still breathless.

"It's a miracle, Young One," Old Ragged whispered. He folded his paws together and gazed with moist eyes.

" And if it wasn't for you, Young One, I would never have seen this amazing tree. I wouldn't have believed it—couldn't have imagined it."

"It must have some special meaning, Uncle."

"Yes. Something very important to the humans," Old Ragged said softly.

XI.

SPRING ON THE HILL

*T*hough they never had to leave their snug home, and seldom did, both Newly and Old Ragged could sense even the subtlest of changes in the weather. They knew that winter was slowly melting into spring, and Newly in particular began feeling the urge to be outside in the sweet, clear air. One afternoon he decided to go scouting for something fresh, or at least different, to add to their supper.

The warm spring sun had melted most of the dirty patches of remaining snow, and tender green shoots of new life poked up everywhere. He scooted across the open space to the hedge, then, for no reason in particular, headed for the old stone wall. Running along its crumbled edge, he suddenly realized he was close to the gooseberry thicket at the bottom of the hill. He hadn't been down this way for a very long time, and he had an almost nostalgic feeling. But something didn't seem quite right.

He scooted down the old passageway and into the burrow where their nest had been. It was littered with soggy leaves and pebbles, washed in by rain and melting snow. It was muddy and damp and not at all inviting. *Funny,* he thought to himself, as he looked around for any signs that they had once lived here. *We never mention our old nest.* He checked for the old escape passage and discovered it had caved in. Then he whisked out into the sunlight and scurried along the ditch at the side of the road, back up the hill.

"I was down by the gooseberry thicket today, Uncle," Newly said later, while they were getting some late-afternoon sun under the hedge. "Long time since we've been there."

"Hmmmmm." Ragged made his usual response. Then he added, "Anything left?"

"Nope. And I was just thinking. There's really nothing to go back down there for. It's so much better up here on the hill."

"True enough, Young One." Old Ragged's tone grew serious. "I've been thinking about that, too. It does seem we have lived here without having the difficulties I expected."

"It has been a wonderful winter," Newly offered. "The best we've ever had."

"Yes. Remarkable," Ragged agreed.

"Soon the earth will be soft enough for Honey to dig a garden," Newly went on. "And the windmill will be pumping water again." He sighed. "Then there'll be long, warm summer evenings when the humans use that fire outside behind the house and leave the delicious drippings in the grass."

"I've never tasted those," Ragged said. "But I wonder if the small human will come back in the summertime and bring that little house?"

"Or if they will bring another tree into the house and make it so beautiful?" Newly added.

They sat, each remembering. Then Newly said, "And Uncle, you have to taste cheese."

"Humph." Old Ragged looked stern. "I have, Newly Born, I have. I know the dangers of cheese very well." He softened. "But no need to talk about that now."

Newly stretched and stood up in the shadow of a low branch. He looked across the yard and beyond to the crest of the hill. The big weathered fan of the old windmill was slowly turning in the breeze.

❧